Published in the United States of America by Crown Publishers, Inc.,
225 Park Avenue South, New York, New York 10003.
Published in Great Britain by Walker Books Ltd.,
184-192 Drummond Street, London NW1 3HP
CROWN, IT'S GREAT TO READ! and logo are trademarks of
Crown Publishers, Inc.
Manufactured in Italy

Library of Congress Cataloging-in-Publication Data
Carter, Anne. Bella's secret garden. Summary: While munching on
lettuce in the Pringles' garden, Bella the rabbit is carried
by a cat to a neighboring meadow, where she discovers other rabbits
and a safer place to feed. 1. Rabbits—Juvenile fiction.
[1. Rabbits—Fiction] I. Butler, John, 1952–   ill. II. Title.
PZ10.3.C28Be   1986   [E]   86-4604
ISBN 0-517-56308-8

10 9 8 7 6 5 4 3 2

First American Edition

BELLA'S
SECRET GARDEN

Written by ANNE CARTER
Illustrated by JOHN BUTLER

CROWN PUBLISHERS, INC., NEW YORK

Bella had never known the meadow. It vanished before she was born. First the bulldozers came and then the builders. Now, only the oldest rabbits could remember a time before the houses were there.

They had to dig a new warren
in piles of earth the builders left.
The older rabbits grumbled.
    But Bella liked it. She liked
the gardens, where peas and
carrots and heads of lettuce were
beginning to grow.

Early morning was the time for gardens. Later, when dreadful dogs came barking out of doors, rabbits ran for their lives. Bella ran happily with the rest. She was quick, clever and safe.

Bella was greedy, too.
The other rabbits rested in the
daytime but Bella found a
secret garden of her own. She
crept off there when nobody
was looking, for a munch of
crisp new lettuce.

And that was how the Pringles'
cat, taking her midday stroll,
happened on the fat young rabbit
sitting up bold as brass in the
middle of the lettuce bed.
   Puss padded closer.

Bella was crunching juicy
lettuce when Puss pounced.
Bella screamed. A masterful
paw held her down. Bella
froze in terror.

But the grip that took her
by the scruff did not hurt.
Bella was lifted off the ground
and hung easily, like a kitten,
as Puss carried her toward
the house.

"Naughty Puss! Poor bunny!
Put it down!"
Puss did. She had meant it for
a present anyway.

Bella hopped once, twice.
Sun was on her back. She was
alive! Then human smell came
around her. Human paws held her.
A deep voice boomed, "You keep
that pesky bunny out of my lettuce!"

"Yes, Dad. It's going in my bike
basket."

Bella sat in a nest of straw
that lurched and swayed.
Nothing was still or safe.
Sunshine and shadow flickered
by. Speed steadied to a gentle
rocking. Bella went to sleep.

The rocking stopped. Bella was on the ground. When she looked around she was alone. The world was filled with sweet green grass. No lettuce. No houses. And no rabbits.

Bella felt strange and lonely.
The afternoon went very slowly.
Then, suddenly, it was evening
playtime, and the field was full
of rabbits. Friendly noses were
twitching, friendly ears flicking.
Happily, Bella went to join them.